Bianca

bratz ™

KEEPIN' IT REAL!

A NOVEL BASED ON BRATZ: THE VIDEO!

By Yasmin™
with Charles O'Connor

*Based on the screenplay by Meg Martin,
Norah Pierson, and Charles O'Connor*

Grosset & Dunlap • New York

For my mother, my sister, and my aunt
—Charles

Executive Brand Editor, Charles O'Connor
TM & © 2004 MGA Entertainment, Inc. Bratz and all related logos, names and distinctive likenesses are the exclusive property of MGA Entertainment, Inc. All Rights Reserved.

Used under license by Penguin Young Readers Group. Published by Grosset & Dunlap, a division of Penguin Young Readers Group, 345 Hudson Street, New York, New York 10014. GROSSET & DUNLAP is a trademark of Penguin Group (USA) Inc. Printed in the U.S.A.

Library of Congress Cataloging-in-Publication Data

O'Connor, Charles.
  Keepin' it real! / by Yasmin ; with Charles O'Connor.
    p. cm.
"Bratz."
"A novel based on Bratz: the video!"
"Based on the screenplay by Meg Martin, Norah Pierson, and Charles O'Connor."
Summary: The girls are nervous about the upcoming prom, and someone is writing unflattering things about them in the school newspaper.
  ISBN 0-448-43365-6 (pbk.)
[1. High schools—Fiction. 2. Schools—Fiction.] I. Title: Keeping it real!. II. Title.
PZ7.O2175Ke 2004
[Fic]—dc22

2003022189

ISBN 0-448-43365-6   A B C D E F G H I J

A QUICKIE INTRODUCTION BY YASMIN!

When Mr. Del Rio, our art teacher, gave my friends and me a last-minute assignment, at first we freaked! I mean, not only was it like the last two weeks of high school before summer, but it was also the last week before the coolest night of the year, Prom! All Cloe, Sasha, Jade, and I wanted to do was cruise and do all the things we had dreamed about doing during the countless tests, term papers, and long nights studying. After all, we had worked hard to finish with flying colors. We definitely deserved it, right? So when we decided on a kickin' cool way to complete our last-minute requirement, we thought our worries were over. But, boy, were we wrong!

Now maybe you've seen our video and, if you have, you know exactly what I'm talking about. But what you don't know is that Mr. O'Shea, my creative writing teacher, said that if I wanted to earn a lil' extra credit, I could write the novelization based on our video project.

3

Obviously, I jumped at the chance! I mean, extra credit or no extra credit, this would be my first-ever book! How cool was that? They always say that behind every great movie, there's an even greater book. Well . . . I guess this is it!

So here we go! Grab yourself a strawberry smoothie, kick up your feet, and read on. You're about to spend a week in the life of my friends and me. It was a crazy time, for sure, but one you can bet we'll never, ever forget.

—YASMIN
XOXO

chapter one

It was the best of times. It was the worst of times. It was less than a week until the most funkadelic night of the year: Prom Night. Outside her house, Cloe sat parked in her new silver-blue Cadillac convertible, brushing her golden blonde hair and touching up her ruby-red lips with a dash of Violet Flare lip gloss. Decked out in faded hip-hugger blue jeans, a brown top, and a stylish tight-fitting jacket, she just couldn't wait to see the look on her friends' faces as she picked them up for school! It had taken months and months of hard work and saving, but now the vintage cruiser was hers.

"Funkalish!" Cloe blurted to her reflection in the mirror. Strapping on her seatbelt and putting the car into drive, she sped away, hubcaps spinning and engine revving. It was time to pick up her girls and get the party started.

Cloe drove through the neighborhood, thinking how cool the week ahead of her was going to be. Everything had been strategically planned by Cloe and her friends so not a moment would be wasted. All of the term papers and tests, all of the projects and reports, seemed like yesterday's news. All that mattered now was Prom. A stylin' slumber party, a visit to the Salon 'N' Spa, even a day at the beach, were all on the roster for making the Prom the biggest night of the year. The only challenge at this point was finding the perfect outfits! Although they were cutting it kinda close, they knew that the perfect mix 'n' match, cutting-edge fashion looks were out there somewhere. And all they had to do was find them!

As Cloe turned the corner, she saw her brown-haired friend Yasmin already making her way to the curb to be picked up, cell phone in hand, smiling from ear to ear. Wearing a stylin' retro jacket with capri-blues, she was the epitome of gorgeous.

"Jade, you're not going to believe the car Cloe bought," Yasmin shouted into the phone, nearly waking the neighborhood in her wicked elation. Yasmin climbed into the stylin' vehicle and ran her hand across the dashboard.

"It may be old, but it's definitely BOLD," responded Cloe, hitting the gas so Jade could hear the massive *vroom-vroom* of the engine through the phone. Putting the car into drive, Cloe checked first to see if the coast was clear, and then she and Yasmin sped away.

"I can't believe how cool this ride is!" Yasmin said to Cloe as she reached for a small notebook and pen and began writing something down.

"What'cha writing?" asked Cloe curiously.

"Oh, nothing!" responded Yasmin. Cloe and the girls knew that Yasmin loved to write, but they also knew how shy she could be about sharing her work with the group. When Yasmin was ready, she would share.

It took only moments to reach Jade's stylish house. Looking up at Jade's room, with its dazzlin' designer curtains in the windows, it was easy to see just how in-style and ahead-of-the-game Jade was, even if you had never had the pleasure of meeting her. Jade was known as the girl who took the greatest style risks at Stiles High.

And it always paid off. She had a knack for predicting fashion trends well before their time. But, best of all, she had a cool, funky personality to match that made her both totally approachable and fun to be with.

From her bedroom, Jade watched Cloe and Yasmin drive up her curvy cool driveway. Opening her window, she yelled hello to the girls, and threw her backpack into the backseat of Cloe's new car. Within moments, Jade came out, wearing burgundy velour pants and a retro funkadelic blue sweater-jacket. She hopped into the backseat and was instantly awed by the leather interior.

"Rockin' ride, Cloe!" said Jade in her raspy, animated voice.

"Let's book!" said Yasmin as the three drove away to pick up Sasha.

Minutes later, the girls pulled up to a house on the west side of town and found cocoa-skinned Sasha sitting on her front stoop, cell phone in hand and deep in conversation. She looked divine in her golden-brown suede jacket and blue capris.

"No, no. 'Mad snacks' means light finger foods.

Nothing too-too heavy. We want them to get up and dance, not get down and go to sleep." Looking up, Sasha's gorgeous eyes widened as she caught a glimpse of the stylin' ride that was now waiting for her. She hung up and made her way over to the car. "Cloe, this so beats taking the school bus!"

"I know what you mean. I hate how I look in yellow!" joked Cloe.

"Prom is gonna be better than ever, now that we've got wheels to cruise in," Jade spoke up.

Sasha glanced over at Jade and gave a shrug as she jumped into the backseat. "Let's hope, girl. I'm working on it."

Everybody knew that Sasha was head of the Prom Committee. And everybody knew just how stressful it could be. Sasha took the gig because she wanted to make this year's Prom even better than it had been in the past. And if anybody could do it, it was Sasha.

"Well, let's jam, then! First bell rings in like three minutes!" yelled Yasmin.

As they raced off, Cloe was about to turn down the

main thoroughfare to school when suddenly she heard a low-vibrating thunder. The girls looked at one another because they knew it could be only one thing: the roar of their good friend Cade's motorcycle. It took only a moment for the girls to catch a cooled-out Cade in a leather jacket and jeans, bandana and boots, and stylin' shades, biking it to school.

"Sweet wheels, Cloe!" shouted Cade as he passed the girls and then sped away.

"Prom Week, here we come!" yelled Cloe as she and the girls made their way to school in what was sure to be the coolest week of their lives.

■　　■　　■　　■

Later that morning, Cloe, Yasmin, Jade, and Sasha found themselves in the only class they all shared together: Mr. Del Rio's art class. Now, normally art class means painting pictures and sculpting clay. But Mr. Del Rio's art class was very different. Sometimes you got to do that stuff, but in general it was more about the listening and less about the doing. Most of the time, the girls would sit for forty-five minutes while Mr. Del Rio would pontificate about art history, which generally translated into long and boring lectures on the history of say, watercolor in the thirteenth century.

Today was no different. For forty minutes, Mr. Del Rio, with his scruffy goatee and checkered cap, stood and spoke about the joys of self-expression in art throughout history. As always, it had the potential to be a fascinating topic—that is, in anybody else's hands.

"Now remember, class, throughout history, artists have used a variety of mediums to express themselves," Mr. Del Rio said. "Van Gogh used paint and canvas, Mozart used music . . ."

"And Gucci used fabric and scissors!" shouted Jade abruptly.

"Yes, thank you, Jade," responded Mr. Del Rio in a less-than-impressed tone. "Now, class, here is the assignment: I want you to choose an artistic medium, any medium, and express yourself."

The class murmured excitedly.

"The project you turn in should tell me who you are

and what it's really like to be you," Mr. Del Rio said.

"I express myself daily, through my passion for fashion," sang Cloe.

"Perhaps you should challenge yourself to find a new medium, Cloe," said Mr. Del Rio.

"Can we work in groups?" asked Sasha.

"As long as each person is equally represented, I don't see why not," Mr. Del Rio replied.

The girls gave a silent "yeah," knowing that this meant they could do the assignment together, making it four times as funkadelic. Finally, something cool to do for Mr. Del Rio's class, the girls thought! For once, art class didn't seem all that bad. But just as the class bell rang, Mr. Del Rio dropped a bomb that would change their minds.

"And . . . oh . . . the assignment is due first thing next week." The girls stopped dead in their tracks. "And it's worth one quarter of your grade in the class."

"What?" blurted Cloe.

"No way!" shouted Jade.

"But Prom is on Saturday, Mr. Del Rio!" pleaded Yasmin.

"That's five days away!" exclaimed Cloe.

"Prom's our top priority this week!" exclaimed Sasha.

"My priorities are classroom activities, not after-school ones. I'm sure you'll find a way to make it work," Mr. Del Rio said sternly.

Bummed out beyond words, the girls shuffled out of Mr. Del Rio's art class in shock and dismay. This was Prom Week. Everything was clear for takeoff. This assignment would ruin everything. It was a fashion disaster.

chapter two

Cloe, Yasmin, Jade, and Sasha slowly made their way to their lockers.

"What Mr. Del Rio isn't hip to is that this week, Prom is what we're about!" exclaimed Sasha.

"He's totally asking us to split focus!" said Jade.

Standing beside their lockers, only a few feet away, good friends Cameron and Dylan could see that the girls were upset about something.

"What's cracking, ladies?" asked Dylan in his usual casual-cool tone.

"We've got a big project due in Mr. Del Rio's class, and it's gonna rob us of valuable Prom prep time!" responded Cloe.

"Oh, bummer!" said Cameron, a good-looking guy with a charming smile and pleasant voice.

"I don't know why y'all are freakin'!" said Sasha,

brushing her long brown hair in front of her locker mirror. "I'm the leader of the Prom Committee, so I'm the one who's gotta hook the whole thing up by Saturday."

"You ladies won't want to miss out on seeing my Prom getup," said Dylan, missing the point. "Lucky for you, we're all going as a group so you'll each get to have at least one dance with me."

"We gotta focus, Hot Stuff!" responded Jade abruptly as she jokingly flung open her locker *into* Dylan, catching him off-guard. "Now, there has to be a way to get out of the assignment."

"Why?" asked Cameron. "Knowing you girls, you'll figure out how to do all your Prom prep AND ace the assignment."

"If only we could find a way to make Prom part of the assignment," exclaimed Sasha.

"I know . . . but how?" asked Cloe, applying a touch of frosty lip gloss to her pouty lips.

A moment of silence came over the group.

"We could . . . no . . . that's stupid," said Yasmin shyly.

"What?" asked Jade curiously.

"It's nothing . . . never mind," responded Yasmin, lightly brushing some magic mascara onto her beautiful brown eyelashes.

"Spit it out, Yas!" blurted Sasha.

"Really, it's stupid," teased Yasmin once again.

"Okay, already!" interjected Cloe. "How about we . . ."

"I was thinking we could make a video!" interrupted Yasmin. "You know . . . like 'a week in the life' of us girls."

A smile came over the group.

"That's a great idea!" shouted Jade excitedly.

"Really?" asked Yasmin.

"Really truly!" said Cloe.

"Too bad we don't have a video camera," Sasha interrupted, closing her locker in disappointment.

"Never fear, my funky fashion friends, you can borrow one from Koby," Dylan chimed in.

"Yeah, Koby works at the A/V Center. He knows everything about film and video," added Cameron.

"Let's hit, y'all! Time's a wastin'!" yelled Sasha as

she jetted ahead of the girls, down the hallway and around the main corner.

■　　■　　■　　■　♪

Cluttered and complicated would be the only way to describe the Audio/Visual Center where Koby spent most of his spare time at school. Cameras, videotapes, microphones, monitors, editing machines, and tons more filled the packed room. It also tended to be a little bit dim, like a basement.

"I'm sure it's here somewhere," said Koby as he rifled through an old cabinet looking for a video camera that the girls could use. Wearing dark, unfaded jeans and a sporty red-knit top, all he needed was a baseball cap on his head and a director's chair at his side and his look would be complete. As Koby continued to search, the school bell blared in the background.

"Oh, man, we're gonna be late for third period, Dyl!" said Cameron.

"Hate to leave my girls, but . . . we gotta jet!"

teased Dylan as both he and Cameron turned to leave.

Sasha suddenly grabbed Dylan's collar and yanked him back from his speedy exit.

"*Your* girls?" questioned Sasha.

"Whose *what*?" demanded Yasmin.

"I don't think so!" replied Cloe.

"We're nobody's girls!" Jade shot back.

Dylan flashed his irresistible smile and lovingly pinched Jade's cheeks. "Later, Jader!" But before the girls could react, Dylan yanked himself free of Sasha's grasp and zipped out the door to catch up with Cameron.

Just then, Koby appeared from behind a pile of electronic thingamajigs with a camera in hand. "I've found the perfect camera for your project, girl . . . uh . . . ladies." Koby caught himself just in time. "It's a simple point-and-shoot."

"This is gonna be so stylin'!" exclaimed Sasha.

"Thanks, Koby," said Cloe, touched by his need to help them out.

"Well, I do pride myself on knowing my way around the old A/V Center," he replied.

"Did you produce all these films, Koby?" asked Jade, noticing the movie posters on the walls.

"Yup. I've worked on some of the greatest video projects this school has ever seen!" offered Koby, situating himself next to his movie poster accomplishments. "*Glee Club Reloaded: Stars in the Bleachers*. Then there was *Mr. Mellman's Corner: The Principal with Principles*."

"Whoops! Napped through that one," whispered Cloe to Sasha.

"Now I'm working on my best film ever. It's called . . ."

"Ummm . . . Thanks for the hook-up, Koby!" said Cloe, trying to close the conversation gracefully. Cloe knew that once he got started, she and the girls would never leave the A/V Center and would probably miss the next class. And the class after that. And the class after that.

"We gotta go," added Sasha, holding the camera up to say thanks, and picking up on Cloe's cue.

"See ya at the movies!" said Yasmin as all four girls turned and bolted out the door, leaving Koby all alone in front of his posters.

"It's called *The History of Cardboard: Recycling*

Stiles. And it's gonna be a mega-hit for sure," Koby called out, grinning from ear to ear.

■   ■   ■   ■

The girls left the A/V Center in a hurry and rushed down the hallway. Realizing that Mr. Del Rio's project could actually be fun, they were looking forward to becoming the superstylin' stars they were destined to be. Sasha held the camera and began pushing the buttons as Koby had showed her. Feeling confident in her movie-making abilities, and just a little inspired by Koby's accomplishments, she put the camera up to her eye and pressed the record button. A red blinking light came on.

"I think it's recording," she said, moving the camera over all the girls, one by one.

"Make sure you cover me from my best side, Bunny Boo," demanded Cloe like a big movie star.

Looking down, Jade realized that she had not prepared for her onscreen debut. "Does this outfit 'read' on film?" she asked.

"Looks pretty good to me," responded Sasha, going

in for an extreme close-up on Jade's velvety number.

"Cut!" yelled Jade suddenly. "I need to head into wardrobe for my big debut!"

Sasha lowered the camera and switched it off. "It's gonna be a long week," she joked under her breath.

chapter three

Approximately an hour later, the girls regrouped for lunchtime at a spacious table in the Stiles High cafeteria.

"This camera is going to dish us the best project in class," said Sasha, holding the camera and feeling less stressed than she was earlier.

"Looks like the *Stiles Shout-Out!* is already 'dishing' big time!" squealed Yasmin in response as she handed the paper to Cloe. "Check the new column."

Cloe grabbed the paper and read the front-page headline to herself. "Countdown to Prom," it said, and included a picture of Sasha with the inscription "Prom Committee Chair" underneath. "Look at you, girl! Front page and everything!"

Sasha placed the camera down and gave a curious smile.

"Turn the page," Yasmin said to Cloe, wanting her to check out the new gossip column.

" 'Daily Doings,' written by Anonymous . . . oooh, mystery much!" exclaimed Cloe as she handed the paper over to Sasha.

"About time! This paper has been crying out for a gossip column!" Jade blurted out.

"Just gimme the scoops!" said Sasha as she began reading. "Mr. Feeney is starting an after-school badminton club . . . the science lab is getting a new shipment of beakers . . . the upper-class parking lot will be expanded over the summer." Sasha looked at the paper with disdain. It was like having just bought a crummy CD that everybody said was the bomb . . . but wasn't. "Fascinating! Anonymous sure got the scoop of the century with that one."

"Yaaaawnnnnski," yawned Cloe. "Daily *Dozings* is more like it. Hope there's better stuff in tomorrow's column."

Sasha threw the paper down. "Yeah, there's gotta be more interesting stuff than this going down at Stiles High."

Yasmin nodded her head in agreement.

"And I think it's coming in to focus as we speak," giggled Jade as she grabbed the video camera and put it up to her eye. "Which one of you is ready for your close-up?"

"I am!" shouted Cloe, jumping up before any of the other girls could respond.

Jade pressed the power button and looked through the viewfinder to catch Cloe in focus.

"How do I look?" asked Cloe.

"Great, but you'd look better against a different color background. Cafeteria brown is definitely not a Cloe color!" responded Jade.

"Then shut that thing off!" demanded Cloe.

"Let's take it out to the football field. The natural light will make you shine, girl!" offered Jade.

"I like the way you think!" Cloe smiled.

■   ■   ■   ■

Minutes later, Jade and Cloe were standing in the bleachers overlooking the football field. "And . . . action!"

Jade yelled, camera in hand, in full directorial mode.

Cloe stared directly into the camera, crystal blue eyes shining. "Hi. I'm Cloe. But you can call me Angel, cuz that's what I am," she declared, and then found herself at a loss for words. "What else should I say?"

"Ummmm . . . tell us about yourself," Jade instructed.

"Well, I'm all about expressing myself through my personal style, flashy attitude, and most importantly, fashion! I love to paint and draw." Cloe smiled as she grabbed her school notebook from the bleachers next to her and began flipping through it, showing the camera her latest artwork and fashion designs. "I love to shop at the mall with my friends." Cloe leaned in to the camera for a confessional. "I love school . . . though we get waaaay too much homework!" she exclaimed. "What else?" Leaping to her feet, Cloe continued. "Oh, yeah! I think there should be a bottled water machine in the cafeteria, and more mirrors in the girls' room. Who knows, maybe next year I'll run for student body president and I'll make that part of my platform. But I can't focus on that now. This is a very important week. Prom is on Saturday! And we've got a lot of work to do if we want to do it in style!"

"Cut!" shouted Jade. "That was really good!"

Cloe beamed. This last-minute art assignment was definitely going to be off the hook.

■　　■　　■　　　■

The school gymnasium was changing. Blossoming. No longer the dingy, dirty, sweaty-smelly place of phys. ed. days and basketball nights, it was undergoing a major makeover thanks to Prom Chair Sasha. In less than a week, the gym would be decorated with flowing banners, psychedelic lights, funky floral designs, and balloons. Tons and tons of balloons. Prom Night would be one night that Stiles High would never forget. And it was Sasha's job to make sure everything went off without a hitch.

Today, things were in full swing. The Prom Committee, consisting of several close friends, was busy unpacking decorations. Having just arrived unannounced, Cloe was hoping to add a little drama to the video assignment by possibly catching a glimpse of Sasha under pressure. But even under major pressure, Sasha was the level head of the bunch and always appeared to be in control. Today was no exception.

"Hey, girl, got a minute?" yelled Cloe to Sasha, who was at the helium tank inflating balloons. "I'm here to record the deep thoughts of our Prom Committee Chair."

Sasha approached Cloe and broke it down in a way only she knew how. "Alright, I'm Sasha, but my friends call me Bunny Boo, cuz I just love the hip-hop thang. But don't get me wrong, I dig all types of music. And I'm into funky threads, kicking it with my buds, and a good challenge, which is one of the reasons I volunteered to be the chairperson of this year's Prom Committee."

Sasha inflated a balloon on the nearby machine and handed it to a red-headed stunner dressed in a white-hot top and pink pants. "Meygan, tie those to the Prom Queen's throne."

Sasha turned her attention back to Cloe and the camera she was holding. "The Prom theme I chose is called 'Formal Funk.' As you can see, I've got my team doing a bang-up job." Sasha gestured to the students behind her unpacking decorations and hanging them from the ceiling.

"Eitan's settin' things up for the kickin' DJ we hired,"

Sasha reported as she glanced at the cute-looking guy in an orange shirt, plugging in lighting cables in the background.

"Nevra's organizing the refreshment table and we've ordered the maddest food around!" Sasha continued, now pointing to a dark-haired beauty in a blue-velvety outfit, setting up the refreshment stand.

"And over there . . ." Sasha said as she pointed to a gorg brown-haired girl wearing red who was setting up amazing floral decorations, ". . . that's Dana decoratin' the backdrop. We've even got a professional fashion photog who's going to come and take everyone's picture. This Prom is gonna be off the hook!"

Just then, two delivery men arrived carrying a huge trellis arch, the regal arch that would hang above the heads of the Prom King and Queen as they received their crowns come Prom Night.

Sasha, realizing that this "interview" was now over, called to her team. "Let's hit it, y'all!"

Cloe lowered the camera and smiled. "Great job, Bunny Boo! Such the professional!"

Sasha smiled warmly as if to say "thanks," but

suddenly caught sight of Dana once again. "Dana, don't just throw the flowers. They've got to be arranged!" she said with a laugh. Cloe knew that under Sasha's direction, this really was going to be a night they would never forget. Cloe could hardly wait.

■   ■   ■   ■

Since Yasmin loved to write, where better for Sasha to capture her on video expressing herself than in one of Yasmin's favorite private hangouts: the computer lab. Yasmin would sometimes sit for hours banging out all those intimate musings that were swimming around in her head 24-7. She definitely was an artist at heart. And this, some considered, was her studio.

As Sasha was fiddling with the doodads on the video camera, Yasmin was finishing up an instant message to her good friend Dana. As soon as she clicked send on the computer, Yasmin swung her swivel chair around and stopped herself dead-set in front of Sasha and her camera.

"Action, Pretty Princess," whispered Sasha as she focused the camera on Yasmin's golden skin.

"Pretty Princess is my nickname, but my real name's Yasmin. I recently moved here, and I was really nervous about fitting in, but I feel like the luckiest girl in the world to have made the best friends ever!" began Yasmin as she suddenly swiveled back in front of the computer and pressed a button. "I love hanging out with Sasha, Cloe, and Jade," Yasmin continued as pictures of the girls instantly appeared onscreen. "We have sleepovers and even ski trips," she added as more candid shots of the girls appeared onscreen. "Come to think of it, we do just about everything together!" Yasmin whipped back around and engaged the camera once again. "I also love to read, especially mystery novels."

Suddenly, the nearby printer began to print.

"What's that you're printing out?" asked Sasha inquisitively, not noticing that Yasmin had hit print after her onscreen presentation.

"Oh, this? It's just an assignment for English class."

Sasha lowered the camera and thought to herself a sec.

"English class? We don't have an assignment due," responded Sasha, confused.

"I meant creative writing class," Yasmin quickly answered back as she turned her face away from Sasha to shut down the computer.

"You are always writing something, girl. You ought to try and get published."

"Yeah," responded Yasmin.

Suddenly, the class bell rang through the building. Grabbing her books, Yasmin stood up. "There's the bell. Gotta jet!"

chapter four

With summer fast approaching, the weather throughout the city was totally hot, which was totally cool. Cloe, Yasmin, Sasha, and Jade loved to spend long afternoons at the beach, taking in the salty air, stylin' sunshine, and smolderin' sand. It was *the* place to just chill out and get horizontal, and with now only four days until Prom, the girls decided a visit was definitely in order to work on the perfect tan. Besides, how could the girls turn in a true-to-life self-expression video without filming a quickie visit to one of their all-time favorite hot spots?

"The next day, the girls are at the beach. Wide-angle sweeping shot of the sand, the surf, the horizon," Jade narrated dramatically, aiming the camera in the direction of a visiting seagull on the distant shore, when suddenly she was interrupted by a loud voice.

"Hey, Spielberg! Aren't you forgetting something?"

Quickly, Jade turned the camera to find Sasha on a beach blanket with Yasmin and Cloe, surrounded by a soda cooler, fashion mags, and bottles of sunscreen.

"Like the stars of your movie?" barked Cloe, who was sketching in her notebook.

"I was just . . . uh . . . just getting an establishing shot!" explained Jade.

"Well, establish yourself over here, will you?" Sasha blurted out.

Jade returned to the girls, this time catching a better glimpse of Cloe's sketch. It was of the nearby sand and surf. "Wow, Cloe, you're really good!" she said.

"Thanks!" responded Cloe humbly as she turned to look at Jade and caught sight of the camera directly on her. "Wait, let me try that again." Grabbing a nearby scarf and wrapping it around her neck and ruby-red bathing suit, Cloe eyed the camera directly and said dramatically, "Thank you, from the bottom of my heart!"

Suddenly, from seemingly out of nowhere, a beach towel flew through the air and landed smack dab on Cloe's head, drooping over her face. Jade burst out laughing and lowered the camera.

"You guys ruined my shot," Jade said as she turned to the scene-stealer, Sasha.

"Sorry, Kool Kat, but Angel won't quit frontin'!" responded Sasha.

Cloe smiled slyly and removed the towel from her head.

"Yeah. This video's supposed to be the real deal. You don't have to prove it to groove it," reminded Yasmin.

Cloe struck an even more dramatic pose. "I say, 'if ya got it, flaunt it'!"

The girls broke out into laughter. Cloe picked up a nearby fashion magazine and began the quest for the perfect fashion outfit. But, after a moment, Prom paranoia began to take hold. "You guys, I'm getting nervous. We're doing great on our video project, but we don't have our outfits picked out. And the Prom's only four days away!"

"Don't worry. We'll pull it off," Sasha replied.

"We always do," confirmed Yasmin as she applied a new layer of suntan lotion to her arms and legs. Yasmin couldn't help but look absolutely stunning in a burgundy bikini with her awesome tanned skin.

Jade grabbed the magazine and began to flip through the glossy pages. Suddenly, a two-piece leather outfit with spandex and lace caught her eye.

"Oooooh! Isn't this all the funk?" Jade asked her friends as she held up the magazine and smiled like she had found a winner.

A pause came over the girls. And then a look to one another.

"Now I know you're tweaked, girl," began Sasha.

"Even for you that's a little over-the-top, Jade," responded Yasmin.

"Yeah, maybe you better go take a dip and cool off," joked Cloe.

Jade turned the magazine around and stared at the outfit she had chosen again. *She* thought it looked super-stylin'. "You really don't think I could work this outfit?" asked Jade.

Cloe, Yasmin, and Sasha looked at one another and shook their heads "no" at the same time.

Just then, Cameron and Dylan—decked out in trunks and T-shirts—raced up and threw their towels down next to where the girls were camped. "Hey, girls," Cameron said, focusing his attention on Cloe.

"What took you so long?" asked Cloe.

"Three chili-cheese dogs, Tsunami fries, and a triple-chocolate malt at the Surf's Up Drive-Thru," responded Dylan as he sipped on a neon-colored twisty straw that came from the huge plastic cup he was holding. "You gals wanna go for a swim?"

"Been there," responded Sasha.

"Done that," added Jade.

"Now we have to research Prom gowns," Cloe informed him, reaching for a handful of fashion mags.

"Oh, yeah? Well, wait till you ladies see the wheels I'm workin' on for the Prom," said Dylan, lowering his shades over his eyes in super-cool mode.

The girls looked curiously at one another.

"Wheels of your own, Dylan?" Yasmin asked.

"They wouldn't, by any chance, be those training

wheels you just took off your bike last week, would they?" joked Jade.

"Laugh if you will, ladies. On Prom Night, you'll be begging to ride with me . . . in style."

Suddenly, Sasha interrupted. "If you all don't mind, no more Prom talk!" The girls looked at one another. "It's only the most stressful assignment I've ever taken on," continued Sasha.

"Bunny Boo-hoo," joked Cloe.

"You definitely need to chill," said Yasmin.

"I'm sorry, guys. This thing is just a lot more work than I expected," Sasha revealed.

"You need cucumbers, girl!" added Jade, forgoing her fashion strikeout only moments before for a little casual-cool compassion. Reaching into the nearby cooler and grabbing a handful of cucumber slices, Jade removed Sasha's sunglasses and placed them over her eyes.

"Ahhh! A no-stress eyeball salad! Now that's relaxing!" said Sasha.

Cameron and Dylan looked at each other. They were

definitely out of their element.

"Come on, Cam. I think this is our cue to leave," suggested Dylan.

"Good idea," responded Cam.

"Have fun relaxin', girls," said Dylan as he kicked off his shoes.

"We will," said Yasmin.

"And watch out for sharks, Dyl!" joked Jade.

"I'll do my best," replied Dylan sarcastically as both he and Cameron jetted down to the roaring waves and sandy beach.

Sharing a laugh, Sasha, Cloe, Yasmin, and Jade turned their attention to the sun as it began its descent into the sea.

■　　■　　■　　■

Hours later, decked out in the cutest after-beach attire, Cloe, Yasmin, Jade, and Sasha were driving home in Cloe's new cruiser. The girls had gotten the footage they needed for the video assignment and had definitely "golded-up" for the upcoming Prom. Now, the sun had set and it was getting a little late. Luckily for the girls, Cloe had her own car to take them home. No more waiting for the city bus.

As Cloe drove down the windy road, Jade sat in the passenger seat. Yasmin was in the backseat with Sasha seated beside her, filming the ride.

"If I do say so myself, the windblown look is awesome for my hair," said Cloe.

"If you don't say it, I will!" responded Jade.

"I just hope I can recreate this style at the Salon 'N' Spa on Saturday," added Cloe.

Suddenly, from out of nowhere, a small black-and-white animal dashed out in front of the speeding cruiser.

"Look out!" shrieked Sasha.

Like a deer caught in headlights, the frightened animal froze in the middle of the road. Cloe jerked the steering wheel to the left and then back to the right. Yasmin, Jade, and Sasha screamed as the car swerved suddenly and narrowly missed the frozen animal. Cloe furiously pressed the brake, but it was too late. The car careened off the side of the road and down an embankment.

Still screaming, the girls braced themselves, as they had absolutely no idea where they were going or how far they were falling. Lipsticks, compacts, suntan lotion bottles, sunglasses, and even the video camera were hurled into the air and back into the cruiser again. And then, as quickly as it had all happened, it stopped. The girls opened their eyes to a plume of smoke and a hiss coming from the front of the car.

chapter five

As the smoke began to subside, the girls looked around. Just in front of them stood a huge oak tree that must've been over one hundred years old. Their car, forced up against it, was now residing in a huge ditch in the middle of the darkened forest.

"Everybody okay?" asked Cloe.

The girls opened the car doors and slowly filed out.

"Yeah, I'm fine," whispered Yasmin.

"Haven't had a ride like that since the Screamin' Meanie Coaster at Funland," said Jade.

"Next time, I drive," asserted Sasha.

Cloe approached the front of the car. "Ohhh! My car!" she cried.

Jade approached the front of the car. "I bet it's not as bad as it looks."

"I don't know. It looks pretty bad," Yasmin confirmed.

"Come on. Let's pick up our stuff," Jade interrupted, leading Yasmin away before she said anything else that might upset Cloe.

Following the path of the runaway cruiser, Yasmin and Jade gathered the things that had flown out of the car during its descent. Make-up, magazines, and snack bags were but some of the items that were now scattered on the newly-made forest trail. Yasmin spotted her sunglasses and picked them up. Even though they were totally bent and out-of-shape, she placed them over her eyes.

"Someone call the fashion police," joked Sasha at the sight of Yasmin.

Sasha noticed the video camera lying on the floor in the backseat. "Oh, no! The camera!" Sasha yelled while picking it up off the ground.

Yasmin, Jade, and even Cloe gathered around. Would it still be working? Although the state of the car was super-important, so was the camera, since it had been entrusted to the girls by Koby. A broken video camera could mean an extra summer job for all the girls just to cover the cost.

"Koby's gonna kill us!" said Jade.

"The way Cloe drives, maybe that won't be necessary," joked Sasha.

"Hey!" snapped Cloe.

Grabbing the camera away from Sasha, Yasmin pressed the power button. A beeping sound could be heard from the camera, followed by a blinking light.

"Luck out. It's not broken." Yasmin pressed the rewind button on the camera. "Maybe we can see what that was in the road."

"It just came out of nowhere!" Jade responded excitedly.

"I think it was a Chihuahua," declared Cloe.

A pause came over the girls as they realized that they didn't know what that thing in the road had been. They looked at one another. And then all four girls looked around at their darkened surroundings and realized something else. They were in the middle of nowhere, deep in the desolate woods. All alone.

"Um, guys, where are we?" Jade asked, her voice cracking a little more than usual.

And then, as if on cue, in the distance, the not-too-far distance, the howl of a coyote (or was it a wolf?) echoed in the darkness. Utter fear enveloped the girls as they huddled close together.

"Oh . . . I . . . think I know where we are," whispered Yasmin.

"Where?" Sasha whispered back.

In the near distance, the surprising crack of branches caused the girls to fling around in spastic terror, only to find nothing there.

"We're . . . at . . ." Yasmin whispered slowly, "the Haunted Elm."

"Ahhhhhhhhhhhhhhhhhhhhhhhhhhhh!!!!!!" screamed Cloe, Sasha, and Jade.

But after only a moment, the girls stopped screaming and looked at one another in silence.

"What's the Haunted Elm?" asked Jade.

"Well, legend has it that Old Man Conroy used to walk out here every night and sit under this very elm tree."

"Uh-huh," responded Cloe, Sasha, and Jade simultaneously, completely mesmerized by Yasmin's story.

Yasmin continued. "And that when the sun sets, you can still find him out here, sitting right underneath it."

"Well, that's good . . . right?" gulped Jade.

"Yeah, maybe he can give us a lift back to town," offered the always-practical Sasha.

"I don't think so," responded Yasmin.

"Why not?" asked Cloe.

"Because Old Man Conroy died fifty years ago!"

"Ahhhhhhhhhhhhhhhhhhhhhhhhhhhhh!!!!!!!" screamed Cloe, Jade, and Sasha.

Suddenly, a strange sound crackled from behind them. A creaking, scratching, unearthly sound. The girls became petrified with fear.

"What's . . ." whispered Cloe.

". . . that . . ." hissed Jade.

". . . sound?" screeched Sasha.

Slowly, the girls turned around to see what it was that was making the terrifying sound. The sound that was now moving closer. As the girls turned fully around, they opened their eyes wide and caught a glimpse of the spellbinding horror that was awaiting them.

"Ahhhhhhhhhhhhhhhhhhhhhhhhhhhh!" they screamed.

But it wasn't horrible at all. In the darkness stood what looked to be a very terrified black-and-white cat.

"Awww . . . it's just a scared kitty. It must've been the same animal from the road. Are you okay, kitty?" asked Jade as she approached the frightened animal and picked it up, nuzzling it close to her cheek.

"We gotta get out of here," exhaled Sasha.

Looking back at the car, Yasmin had an idea. "Maybe we can push the car to a service station."

"We're too far from town. It would take us all night to push it," responded Cloe.

"Let's call Cameron on his cell phone," suggested Jade.

"Good idea. Maybe we can catch him before he leaves the beach," affirmed Cloe.

"He knows all about cars," Jade continued. "I'll bet he'll be able to fix it right up."

"Otherwise, we'll be riding bicycles to Prom," joked Yasmin.

46

A pause fell over the girls.

"Get Cameron on the phone, NOW," urged Cloe desperately, realizing bicycles and Prom should never go together.

Sasha picked up her cell phone from the backseat of the cruiser. She began to dial Cameron's number, walking quite a bit away in her attempt to locate a stronger signal on her cell.

"Would you like to come home and live with me, kitty?" asked Jade.

Suddenly, Cloe's eyes widened and her heart began to pound fiercely. She had seen something that had scared her more than Old Man Conroy ever could have. "Okay, Kool Kat? I'm going to tell you something and I don't want you to make any sudden movements."

Yasmin suddenly turned to look at Jade and became gripped by fear, as well.

"What is it?" asked Jade innocently.

"That kitty cat . . . it's . . . not . . . a . . . cat," whispered Cloe slowly.

Confused, Jade looked down and instantly understood why her friends were looking at her as if they had seen a ghost. Nestled in her arms was not a black-and-white helpless-looking kitty cat. It was a black-and-white SKUNK!

"Ahhhhhhhhhhh!" screamed Jade as she inadvertently threw the skunk in the direction of Cloe. The skunk landed smack dab in Cloe's arms and let out a shot of its spray, nailing Cloe in the chest!

"Ahhhhhhhhhhh!" yelled Cloe as she tossed the skunk back into the air, but this time it was Yasmin who inadvertently caught the now very frightened animal. The skunk once again sprayed his stinky cologne all over Yasmin, who by this time had tossed it back into the air. Landing on the ground, the skunk quickly scurried off, leaving all three girls a smelly mess.

Unaware of the battle that had just been waged, Sasha returned to the girls, cell phone still in hand, in high spirits.

"Good news. Cam's on the way!" announced Sasha, before catching a whiff of the new scent the girls were now sporting. "Yuck! What's that smell?"

Cloe, Yasmin, and Jade refused to respond.

■　　■　　■　　■

As the girls sat in the darkened woods waiting for Cameron to arrive, Yasmin thought to herself how crazy this whole night had been. But, despite totaling Cloe's car, everything since then had been rather funny. Yasmin grabbed the camera and switched it on. *Yep, still working,* she thought as she pointed it at the girls.

"Do you have to point that at me at this very moment, Yasmin?" asked Sasha.

Cloe, looking like a tornado had hit her hair, tried to maintain her composure.

"This day has been very difficult."

"This day was fine, until we had the car accident," responded Jade to Cloe.

"And it's all my fault!" shrieked Cloe, now losing it.

Jade put her arm around Cloe. "No, Angel, it was an accident."

"It could've happened to anyone, Cloe," Sasha

assured her. "Don't be so hard on yourself."

"But we were going to take the cruiser to Prom!"

"Angel, we all had our seatbelts on, and we're all okay," Jade reminded her. "That's what's important."

Cloe knew her friends were right. "You mean it?"

"Yes," Sasha said.

Yasmin, still holding the camera, nodded up and down, as did Cloe's image in the viewfinder.

"Thanks, guys. You're the best," said Cloe as Jade hugged her close. "Wow, you guys smell terrible!"

"So do you," Jade shot back as both girls started laughing.

Suddenly, as if the moment couldn't have been any sweeter, the trees directly opposite the group lit up and shadows began to race across Cloe's cruiser and the girls as they sat there.

"Cameron's here!" yelled Yasmin.

The girls raced toward the embankment where their car had veered off and began to wave their arms frantically. As they did, Cameron's car pulled to the edge of the embankment and stopped. The car doors opened, and

Cameron and Dylan jumped out.

"Cameron . . . we're down here!" yelled Cloe.

Cameron looked down and caught sight of Cloe and the girls. And smiled that boyish smile of his.

"Is everybody okay?" shouted Dylan.

"We're fine, but get us out of here!" yelled Jade.

Cameron and Dylan made their way down to the girls. Jade grabbed the video camera, switched it on, and pointed it toward them. "Gotta get our 'big save' on film!" she said.

But as she did, Cloe jumped in front of the camera and blocked the view of the guys' approach, feeling it was time to add a little more riveting drama to Mr. Del Rio's art assignment. "When we went down the embankment, I thought for sure I was a goner!" Jade pushed the camera in close to give Cloe the extreme close-up she felt she deserved.

"You seem fine now," interjected Cameron, stepping into Cloe's frame.

"Cameron, please!" interrupted Yasmin. "Say you can fix this old hunk of junk for us!"

"Are you kidding? They haven't made a car yet that Cam can't fix!" declared Dylan. He wrinkled his nose. "Hey . . . what's that horrible smell?"

"Don't ask," said Jade.

"Yeah. This is no problem," Cameron said shyly as he inspected the damage to the cruiser. "I'm pretty sure I can fix her up before Prom Night." Hearing the good news, Cloe turned, and both she and Cameron shared a quick smile. Yasmin, Jade, and Sasha grabbed one another and jumped for joy. Things were definitely beginning to look up for them.

chapter six

The ringing of the school bell signaled that another day was over at Stiles High. And what a crazy day it had been. Both Cloe and Sasha were surprised in class with last-minute pop quizzes, quizzes they obviously hadn't prepared for since their cruiser accident fiasco of the night before. Poor Yasmin was only two sentences away from finishing a short story assignment for creative writing class when the power in the computer lab inexplicably went out, erasing nearly all of her original story, and causing her to miss the deadline. And Jade found herself completely embarrassed in drama class when she totally blanked on the Shakespearean monologue she was performing. Up there in front of everybody, without anything to say, she felt like time stood still. And the sudden improv she was forced to do to cover up only made matters worse.

But now all that was over. It was now only three

days to the Prom and, hopefully, the girls thought, Cameron was closer to fixing the cruiser.

"To the mall, girls!" shouted Jade as if giving a victorious battle cry.

"I am going to find the perfect Prom dress if I have to try on everything in the mall," said Sasha, pretty in pink plats and a pink mini.

Yasmin smiled. "Not if I find it first!" she said as she pulled out a page from a fashion mag that she had ripped out during lunch.

"And we can't forget about new make-up!" Cloe reminded the girls. "Jade, you're still doing makeovers on all of us at my slumber party tomorrow night, right?"

Jade pushed ahead, grabbed the school's old wooden front doors, and swung them open for the girls to pass. "Your fashion wish is my command!"

The girls were making their way out of the building when they suddenly noticed small groups of students huddled all around, whispering and snickering, eyes buried in the latest edition of the *Stiles Shout-Out!* Under a nearby tree, their friends Eitan and Meygan were standing, paper in hand, mouths open in shock.

"This is way bad," whispered Eitan to Meygan.

Meygan lifted her head and caught sight of the girls. "Come on!" she said as she grabbed the paper and made a dash for them.

"Hey, wait up!" yelled Eitan, quickly following behind.

Cloe, Yasmin, Sasha, and Jade made their way through the courtyard. As they did, they could feel the nearby students now watching them. And whispering.

"Why do I feel like I just walked out of the bathroom trailing T.P. on my heels?" asked Sasha.

Meygan and Eitan jumped in front of the girls. "Did you guys see today's 'Daily Doings'?" Megan asked as she whipped the newspaper in front of them.

"Everybody else has," informed Eitan.

Jade snapped the paper out of Meygan's hands and began reading out loud. " 'Has Prom Player Sasha lost her grip on the biggest event of the year?' "

"What?" snapped Sasha. "Let me see that!" Sasha lunged for the paper Jade was holding, but as she did, a curious Jade pulled it back and ducked around a nearby flagpole to keep her from snatching it.

" 'Our sources tell Daily Doings that the Prom purveyor is falling apart at the seams!' " Jade continued.

"I am not! And what sources?" questioned Sasha as she lunged once again for the paper, but was too slow for Jade's quick hand.

" 'And maybe she's even heading into full breakdown mode as the big night nears,' " Jade read.

Sasha couldn't believe what she was hearing. She just had to see it to believe it.

" 'The Prom looks to be the hottest night of the year,' " Jade continued. " 'But will our chairperson put her own personal demons aside in time to enjoy the festivities?' " Jade circled around a group of nearby students only to be met finally by Sasha, who quickly grabbed the paper and began reading to herself.

"I am not having a breakdown!!! Who's feeding them this trash?" Sasha blurted out suddenly.

Cloe, Yasmin, and Jade fell silent. As did everybody else in the courtyard.

"Okay, maybe I am stressing a little," Sasha

whispered. "But how does 'Daily Doings' know that?"

Cameron and Dylan were just walking out of the school building when they caught sight of the girls and approached them.

"Hi, guys!" said Cameron.

"Off to the mall?" asked Dylan.

"We were, until I read this," Sasha shot back, holding up the paper to them.

Dylan began to chuckle. "Yeah, we saw that."

"And you know, you *still* seem a little stressed," joked Cameron.

"Maybe you should go get a nice, calming 'food court facial' at the mall," joked Dylan.

"I think we'd better cool it," said Cameron to Dylan.

"*Somebody* told the *Stiles Shout-Out!* about our private conversation at the beach," said Cloe sharply.

"Why are you staring at me?" asked Cameron.

"Who else could've told them what we talked about?" demanded Cloe.

"Wait a sec. What are you saying?" asked Cameron.

"Relax," said Dylan as he quickly grabbed Cameron

and pulled him back, away from the girls. "Nobody takes that column seriously."

"Let's go," said Cameron as he took one last look at Cloe and then left with Dylan.

As the guys took off, the girls realized that they were in the middle of a full-fledged scene. Cloe, Yasmin, Jade, and Sasha turned to one another in a moment of shock. How could the guys they had trusted do this to them? And why? They were the only ones who knew about Sasha's stress-out at the beach. Nobody else did. Things apparently were not what they seemed.

"I can't believe they did this!" said Jade.

Sasha turned to her friends in a moment of vulnerability. "You guys know I'm only stressing because I'm trying to make the Prom the best night of our lives, right?"

"You're not really upset by that column, are you, Sasha?" asked Yasmin.

Sasha thought for a moment. She had been so caught up in everything that she didn't even know how she really felt about it. "Naw. I guess not. I overreacted."

"Right," interjected Cloe. "You're so way above this

kind of thing."

"Yeah! You can't let a stupid column rattle you," said Jade.

"Right. There's no way I'm gonna let some anonymous wannabe newshound get to me. You know me better than that," declared Sasha as she took the school newspaper, crunched it up, and slam-dunked it into a nearby trash can.

"That's the spirit!" Yasmin said.

"Now, let's shop!" announced Sasha.

Without a moment more to lose, Cloe, Yasmin, Jade, and Sasha jetted off to find their dresses for the Prom.

■　　■　　■　　■

A cloud of black smoke billowed up into the sky as the noisy city bus pulled in front of the local mall and stopped. Cloe, Yasmin, Jade, and Sasha stepped out of the bus and turned as it once again exhaled another round of black smoke and made its departure.

"I still can't believe the guys would do that to me," said Sasha.

"I thought you said you were over that already," responded Yasmin.

"Cameron just better have my car fixed by Saturday, in time for Prom," reminded Cloe.

"If not, we'd better shop for some sensible heels," chirped Jade.

"Why?" asked Sasha.

"Because I'm walking to the Prom before I take THAT bus again!"

Less than an hour later, the girls were knee-deep in mix 'n' match heaven at their favorite fashion store, Chix. They were trying on practically everything in sight, in search of the perfect dresses for the Prom.

After trying on several so-so gowns, Sasha grabbed a dress she had found buried on a nearby rack and headed to the dressing room. Moments later, she stood in front of the dressing room mirror and knew she had found the *one*. She turned to her friends to ask them for their opinions. But it was their smiles that said it all. Decked out in a full-length midnight-blue gown, sequined as if from the stars high above, Sasha looked like *she* should've been nicknamed Pretty Princess. Timeless, trendy, and absolutely stylin', all that was missing was a glass slipper. In excitement, she grabbed a nearby mannequin with pal Cloe and pretended to accept the honor of Prom Queen, startling an older woman who just happened to be passing by.

Soon after, it was Cloe's turn to fall in love as she stood in front of the full-length mirror dressed in a chalk-gray and black two-piece. Looking radiant beyond words, she knew she would be the belle of the ball in the classic-cool gown. To top it off, she put on a pair of sparkling earrings while Sasha pulled up Cloe's blonde hair with a silver-sparkly hair clip. *This is it*, Cloe thought. *This is the look*. She was now ready to strut her stuff at the party of the year!

It took only a couple of moments more for Yasmin to piece together the perfect outfit. In a formfitting dark blue gown with floral stitching that looked like it had been lifted off the cover of a French fashion mag circa 1965, she looked sophisticated and stunning. Retro, but oh sooooooo cool! Yasmin felt she was definitely Prom Queen material.

Jade knew she was up next. The other girls

definitely had it going on, but the time had come to up the cool quotient by a thousand. It was time to reveal (and revel in) Jade's Prom look.

Jade called out to the other girls. "You ready to rock?" she asked, knowing she was the one with the winner, for sure.

"Bring it," responded Sasha, ready to be dazzled.

Slowly, Jade opened the curtain. The girls looked on, burning with curiosity. And then . . . after a moment . . . Jade stepped out. And then . . . silence.

"Kool Kat?" asked Sasha in disbelief.

"It's Prom, not Halloween!" Cloe joked.

Jade stood there, dressed in a pink tutu-like skirt, a black top, and gray mishmash nylon stockings.

"What? I just really wanted to make a splash with my Prom outfit!" responded Jade defensively. "You don't like it?"

"Mmmmmm. I don't think so," responded Cloe as she turned to a nearby accessories counter with Sasha and began perusing all of the little shimmering goodies on display.

Totally confused, Jade decided that if her friends didn't like it, then maybe it wasn't that good. Sure, her taste in clothes had always been a little more "out there" than the others, and her independent spirit made it fun to push the envelope on style, but this was clearly a strikeout for them. Jade began to doubt herself. Maybe this look wasn't all that good. Unsure of where she went wrong, Jade headed back to the dressing room to strike her latest look. Yasmin, who had said nothing during the exchange, looked on.

"You think it's too much, too?" Jade asked Yasmin.

"Well, it's kinda like that one you picked out in the magazine at the beach," Yasmin said carefully.

That's right, Jade thought to herself. Her *other* fashion faux pas. "Am I losing my fashion sense?" she said to herself quietly.

Yasmin reached into her bag and pulled out the video camera. "Hey, I should be getting this shopping spree for our project. Especially since you haven't had your feature yet!" Unaware of Jade's sudden vulnerability, Yasmin pointed the camera at her. "You're on, Jade."

Always the tough cookie, Jade bravely turned her attention to the camera. "Okay, I'm Jade, a.k.a. Kool Kat, you know. I'm all about fashion, fun, and most importantly, my friends." Grabbing a nearby hat and placing it atop her head, Jade continued. "I love to take style risks and start new trends." Tossing off the hat, Jade picked up a feather boa from a nearby hanger and flung it around her neck. "Sometimes people think the outfits I put together are too crazy. But my best friends have always supported my vision for hot new styles."

"That was great," Yasmin declared as she lowered the camera. "Let me just check the camera for sound." As Yasmin turned away, Jade turned back to the mirror and stared, her momentary bravado now gone.

"Now it's like . . . it's like . . . I'm beginning to lose my own sense of fashion, for the first time ever!" Jade revealed. Saying these words, she felt like she was in a very bad dream.

"Come on, you two," called Sasha.

"Yeah, let's head over to the food court. I need a food break," added Cloe. "We can come back later and finish up."

Finishing with the camera check, Yasmin put the camera into her bag and looked to Jade. She could see that something was definitely up. "We'll catch up," she yelled back casually, not wanting to make a scene.

As the other girls left the store, Jade turned to Yasmin and opened up. "Yas, if I lost my fashion sense, it would be like losing my sense of vision, or my sense of smell, or touch, or taste! I mean, you guys depend on me for style tips and the hot new trends I find, right?"

"Sure," responded Yasmin. "But we like you because you're such a great friend." Yasmin reached over and hugged Jade. "And this friend says you look like you could use a super yummy fruit smoothie. So, hurry up and change."

Smiling, Jade knew Yasmin was right. And who cared if the girls didn't like her choice. Maybe it wasn't a winner. Maybe it was. *But all that matters*, Jade silently confirmed in true girl-power fashion, *is that I be true to myself*. And that's exactly what she intended to do. Jade closed the curtain and began to change. It was definitely time for a smoothie.

chapter seven

Things were getting good for the girls once again. Not only had all the girls put together the most funkadelic formal-wear looks Stiles High would ever see, but Sasha had spoken to Meygan after school and she confirmed that everything was totally on time and, most importantly, on target for the Prom, which was now only two days away. Yesterday's "Daily Doings" article was yesterday's news.

And despite still having to deal with the boys for leaking a false story to the school paper, the girls decided to focus on the positive. After all, tonight was the night the girls had planned to have a slumber party. It was time to get the party started.

Cloe and Sasha sat dressed in the cutest pink pj outfits. In the kitchen, Yasmin was preparing her tasty treats for the exciting night ahead, while Jade was changing into something cute and comfortable in the bathroom.

Sprawled on the floor were sleeping bags, make-up bottles, fashion mags, soda pop cans, several bags of chips and popcorn, and a dark green bottle of the finest sparkling cider you could buy.

"What better way to express our 'true selves' for Mr. Del Rio's project," Cloe began as she grabbed the camera, "than to show us at one of our famous slumber parties!"

"Hold up, Cloe," Sasha responded as she approached the camera and began talking directly into it. "It's not the real deal until I start cranking the tunes." Reaching into her nearby bag, Sasha grabbed a CD and popped it into her nearby Beauty Boombox. The sound of big breakbeats swirled over an echoing melody, building until a final techno two-step kicked in. Going into full DJ mode, Sasha cranked the music loud and started to bounce in her too-cute blue-and-yellow bunny pj's. "Totally hot. Just dropped yesterday. This is the stuff right here."

"Nice," shouted Cloe.

"Great beat," jammed Jade as she rushed out of the bathroom in colorful blue floral pajamas, and high-fived

Sasha to show that she was feeling the groove. Both girls started to dance wildly. Feeling Cloe's camera on her, Jade put out her hands and began pounding to the beat. She was vogueing, and she looked like a million bucks. Nobody would ever say Jade couldn't cut a rug.

"Jade, you were born to be a star," shouted Cloe over the music.

Suddenly, Jade raced over to the boombox and lowered the volume. Turning to the camera, she grabbed a hairbrush, and as if receiving an award, began to bluster. "I'd like to thank all the people who made this possible, especially my amazing camerawoman, Cloe!"

"Yeah, well, the Amazing Cloe has lost all feeling in her wrist from holding up that camera," said Cloe as she lowered the camera and flopped down on the couch, shaking out her hand to restart the circulation. Spotting the latest edition of the *Stiles Shout-Out!*, Cloe grabbed the paper and began to catch up on all the latest news.

Sasha walked to the bathroom and smiled when she saw, stacked from sink to bathtub, the mounds of hair-care products, perfume bottles, hair clips, astringents, mud packs, cotton balls, and gobs of other beauty products. "As usual, Jade has brought enough hair-care products to make over the entire city!" she yelled.

Cloe ran to the bathroom to see what goodies were waiting for her, and sang in delight. "You're like a fashion superhero, Jade!"

"Where there is dry scalp, where there are split ends, there you shall find me . . . Super-Hair-Care-Gal! Dum-ta-da-dum!" joked Jade.

"Hey, Yas, hurry up with your world-famous guac and chips!" yelled Sasha.

"Yeah, you got girls starving out here," yelled Jade.

From the kitchen, Yasmin called back, "All right! All right! Perfect guacamole doesn't just happen, you know!"

Cloe's eyes suddenly widened as she continued to read the paper. "Um, Jade?" she said, grasping for words. "I think you might lose your appetite when you read the latest 'Daily Doings'."

"Why?" asked Jade.

Cloe held up the paper. "You seem to be the star of today's scandal sheet."

Jade read the headline aloud. " 'Has school fashion pioneer Jade taken a wrong turn on the style superhighway?' "

"Uh-oh, here we go again," declared Sasha.

Jade continued reading. " 'Inside sources confirm that, on a recent mall crawl, the usually trendy Jade was seen trying on outfits that hinted to those in the know that she had become FASHION-IMPAIRED!' " Jade reeled in horror and fell back onto the couch. "Oh, no! I, who have been a fashion leader, am now considered but a fallen fashion star! My worst nightmare has come true!" Jade covered her head with the paper.

"Jade, try to stay calm," said Sasha as she pulled the paper off of Jade.

"No one pays attention to this fluff!" reassured Cloe.

"At least this means Cameron and Dyl are off the hook. There's no way they could've known about the mall," said Sasha.

Just then, Yasmin entered with a tray of her famous guacamole dip and a king-sized bag of chips. "I come bearing food," she said as she set the tray on the coffee table. "Let the pajama party begin!"

Jade grabbed the paper from Cloe and waved it at

Yasmin. "Did you see this?" she asked.

"No, but I hear it's become the hottest column in the paper's history!" said Yasmin.

"You told me no one reads it," Jade shot back to Cloe.

Suddenly, the doorbell rang. Saved by the bell, Cloe jumped up. "I'll get it," she said as she made a hasty getaway. Meanwhile, Sasha and Yasmin looked on.

"What's happening to me?" Jade asked, feeling her forehead in search of a fever. "Maybe I'm really coming down with something." Jade's penchant for drama was in full swing. Suddenly, she was back to questioning her very own judgment, something Jade never used to do.

Cloe approached the front door and looked through the peephole. Standing there wearing a mechanic's jumpsuit covered in oil and grease was Cameron, still managing to look cute under the grime. Cloe opened the door. "Hi, Cameron," she said.

Cameron stepped in slightly and began to speak in a hushed, but determined tone. "Umm . . . Hey, Cloe. Listen. I gotta tell you something."

Before Cameron could get another word out, Cloe

quickly interjected. "Actually, I have something to say to you, too."

"Me first. Look, Dylan and I didn't have anything to do with that article in the *Stiles Shout-Out!* yesterday. You gotta believe us."

"I do," responded Cloe.

Cameron continued. "There's no way we'd ever . . . wait . . . what did you say?"

"We know it wasn't you guys," reiterated Cloe.

"You do? How?" asked Cameron.

"Because Jade got trashed in today's edition," Cloe continued. "And there's no way you could have known about her losing her fashion sense. I'm sorry I blamed you. Can you forgive me?"

"Sure. It's okay. How's Jade taking it?"

"Why don't you ask her?" Cloe grabbed Cameron's hand and began to pull him into the den where the girls were. "Hey, everybody," Cloe announced. "Look what the cat dragged in!"

"Hey, Cam!" shouted Jade.

"Hi!" said Yasmin, munching on her chips.

Sasha stepped forward. "I'm really sorry I went after you so bad yesterday, Cam."

"Yeah, I guess it's someone else feeding the paper all these gossipy tidbits, after all," declared Jade, holding up the latest edition.

"Wow, I didn't realize you were all going to be here. I came to see Cloe," said Cameron shyly.

"Oh?" questioned Jade, now perking up.

"Yeah," smiled Cameron. "Nice jammies."

Suddenly, the girls realized that they were in their pj's! No boy had ever been witness to one of their slumber parties. They jumped into their sleeping bags and covered themselves up with pillows.

"Oh . . . yeah . . . I came to tell you," chuckled Cameron as he turned to Cloe, "that your car is definitely going to be ready for Prom."

"We'll have the cruiser for Prom!" screamed Cloe.

"Well, at least something is going right," responded Jade, abandoning her desperation for the unexpected good news.

"I really think you're gonna like what I've done

with it, too," Cameron added.

"You are the best, Cameron!" declared Cloe.

"Unfortunately, you're also the filthiest," said Sasha, laughing.

"And the scruffiest," added Jade.

"You need the full makeover treatment," suggested Yasmin.

"What?" shouted Cameron as the girls slowly began to surround him.

Jade reached for the video camera and flicked it on.

"We promise it won't hurt," whispered Sasha as she and Cloe pushed him down onto the sofa.

"Wouldn't you girls rather work on each other?" asked Cameron, his voice now shaking.

Yasmin popped a box of tissues and began pulling some out slowly, as if sharpening her weapons of choice. "No, we make over ourselves all the time."

Cloe grabbed a tube of hair gel and began to squeeze some out onto her hand. "A boy makeover will be a great challenge!" she said devilishly.

Grabbing a hairbrush and a comb, Sasha readied herself

for the battle ahead. "Let's go, girls!" she jokingly called to arms.

All at once, Cloe, Yasmin, Sasha, and even Jade moved in on Cameron. Suddenly, tissues began flying in the air. Then a squirt of hair gel could be seen hitting a nearby lamp. But it was the screams of protest from Cameron that indicated Sasha had already gotten to and was working on his hair. There was no getting around it. Cameron was in for a night he was sure to never, ever forget.

■　　■　　■　　■

Hours later, the girls were lying in their sleeping bags.

"What a night!" Jade said to her sleepyhead friends, holding the camera up to her eye and filming the girls. "I'll never forget the look on Cameron's face when he saw the makeover we gave him!"

"Like the saying goes, a picture's worth a thousand words," said Yasmin.

"Well, no more words here, please! I'm beat," Jade responded as she turned the camera she was holding around and looked for the power switch. "How do you turn it off, anyway? Oh, here," she said, pressing a button and placing it down on the table next to the girls. But Jade didn't notice that a faded glow reflected from the back of the camera—the camera was still on! Jade turned off the light and got into her sleeping bag.

Some time later, as the girls were catching their beauty z's and dreaming of just how cool Prom was destined to be, a shadowy figure appeared and began to move in the darkness surrounding the girls. No sound could be heard, but after a moment, the illumination of a small flashlight lit up the room. The figure pulled out what looked to be a notebook and began to write. After a couple of minutes, the figure approached the video camera and picked it up. And then, suddenly, the glow from the camera went black.

chapter eight

It was at lunch, the day before the Prom, when the girls found themselves in the cafeteria surrounded suddenly by a strange commotion. Everybody around them was laughing and shouting.

"What's with all the commotion?" asked Cloe.

"You're not going to believe this," responded Sasha, holding up the latest edition of the *Stiles Shout-Out!* "Anonymous has struck again!"

Cloe grabbed the paper and read the headline aloud. " 'Stiles High Grease Monkey Primps for Prom!' " Just below it was a picture of good friend Cameron wearing a mud pack with thick cucumber slices over his eyes.

"Oh, no," whispered Jade, when suddenly a door slammed open, echoing across the cafeteria. Everybody turned to find Cameron standing in the threshold of the cafeteria's doorway, scanning the crowd. He was looking furious and he was looking for someone. As he spotted Cloe, he made his way over to her table. With each step that he took, he seemed to be getting angrier and angrier. Best friend Dylan was a few feet behind him, doing what only best friends do best.

"Hey, Cam! Can you recommend a blush that'll bring out my eyes?"

"Keep it up, Dyl. And *I'll* bring out your eyes *myself*!" Cameron shot back.

He reached the girls' table. "How did the paper get those pictures?"

"I don't know," responded Cloe.

"Well, you and your friends were the only ones there," he shouted. "And, suddenly, I'm the laughingstock of the whole school!"

"Cameron, I swear . . ." Cloe started.

But Cameron cut her off. "Somebody should come pick up your car, because I'm not going to the Prom!"

Cameron stormed off as the cafeteria continued

its laughter. Cloe collapsed into her seat and did her best to fight off tears.

■　　■　　■　　■

It was about an hour later that the girls found themselves sitting at a table in the school library, glaring at one another suspiciously.

"I just don't get it," whispered Cloe. "We were the only ones at my house last night. We had the camera."

"Are you accusing somebody? Cuz I don't appreciate being accused of stuff I didn't do," snapped Sasha.

Leaning in, Cloe snapped back, "I'm not accusing you. I'm just confused."

"Shhhh . . . the librarian's looking," whispered Yasmin, burying her nose in a book.

"Alright. Who took the camera this morning?" asked Sasha.

"I did," responded Cloe as she reached into her bag and pulled out the camera. "It's right here. But I didn't take it out of my bag all day. The *Shout-Out!* came out first period. It wasn't me!"

Jade spoke up in frustration. "I can't trust my friends, I can't trust my fashion sense. I can't trust anything anymore!" she said as she put her head down on the table.

Cloe turned to Yasmin. "You okay over there, Pretty Princess? You're being awful quiet."

Yasmin shrugged.

"What's wrong?" asked Jade.

"Yeah, what is it? It's not like *you* got slammed in 'Daily Doings'," said Cloe.

"It's not like you did, either, Cloe," reminded Sasha.

"But Cameron blames me for that stupid picture of him, which is practically worse!" Cloe defended herself. "You know . . . come to think of it . . . you've hardly been affected at all by this 'Daily Doings' fiasco, Yasmin."

"And you knew about what I was going through with the Prom prep," added Sasha.

"And you were the only one I confided in at the mall about losing my fashion sense!" added Jade.

"And you had access to the camera last night. You could have downloaded the pictures of Cameron when we were asleep," declared Cloe. "Yasmin?"

All three girls paused a moment, waiting to see if Yasmin had anything to say. Sasha picked up the camera and opened the cassette holder. "The tape is gone!"

"No way!" shrieked Jade.

"Our assignment is gone?" asked Cloe.

"All that work . . ." whispered Sasha in disbelief.

And then, suddenly, Yasmin slid the tape across the table. "Alright! Alright! It was me!"

Cloe, Sasha, and Jade looked at Yasmin in shock.

"You were leaking stories to the 'Daily Doings' mystery writer?" asked Jade.

Yasmin lowered her head. "Worse," she said.

"Yas, how could it be worse?" asked Sasha.

"I *am* the 'Daily Doings' mystery writer!"

Cloe, Sasha, and Jade gasped in horror. How could this be? Yasmin was their best friend. They had trusted her with their insecurities and fears, just as she had done with them. How could she have taken those fears and exploited them? For the school newspaper, even? Yasmin was not the friend she appeared to be.

Hearing the hoopla, a librarian rushed to the girls'

table and began to whisper, "If you girls can't stop talking, I'm going to have to ask you to leave the library."

"That's okay, we were just leaving anyway," responded Cloe as she, Sasha, and Jade got up out of their seats, turned their backs on their so-called best friend Yasmin, and stormed out of the library. Yasmin covered her face with her hands and sank back into her chair.

chapter nine

The Stylin' Salon 'N' Spa. Not just a place for the latest and greatest cutting-edge fashion hairstyles from some of the coolest hairdressers in town, it's also a place of delicious pampering. French manicures and delicate pedicures are always on the menu. So are make-up makeovers from the world's greatest fashion mags. And there's always time for a dip in the bubbly beauty Jacuzzi that is filled to the brim with everything from steaming floral-scented water to slices of tropical fruit. Now with the Prom only hours away, a visit to the Salon 'N' Spa was only the beginning of the long-awaited party for Cloe, Jade, and Sasha. It was everything they could ever possibly want or need for looking and feeling beautiful. But something was definitely missing.

"This is ridiculous," said Cloe as she jumped up from her slumped sitting position, decked out in a robe, hair curlers, and a mud pack.

Jade, soaking her nails for a manicure, seconded the motion. "We're at the spa . . ."

"The one place in the whole world where we always have fun," Sasha continued, her hair wrapped up in a towel and her feet drowning in a hydro-massager.

"Our private beauty boot camp," declared Cloe.

"Our mud-pack makeover mecca," finished Jade.

"And we're having a miserable time," sighed Sasha.

"Because Yasmin's not with us!" proclaimed Cloe.

"And Prom is going to be even worse without her," continued Jade.

Cloe began to pace the room, stopping beside her best friends Sasha and Jade and putting her arms around them. "We have to talk to her, guys! After all, we're the ones who said we wanted the school paper to print juicier stories, right?"

"Yasmin sure delivered on that!" exclaimed Sasha.

"Got that right," confirmed Jade, thinking back to only yesterday when she was convinced that she had lost her fashion sense, but now realizing that she had just been caught up in the moment.

"Hey . . . we *were* the talk of the school all week," smiled Cloe.

"Yeah, and like the old saying goes: 'Who cares what they write, as long as they spell our names right'," joked Jade.

Cloe, Sasha, and Jade began to laugh together for the first time in over a day. But, suddenly, the sound of the salon door opening echoed through their beauty chamber and caught their attention. Turning, the girls looked to see who it was and were flabbergasted by who they saw: It was their best friend. It was Yasmin.

"Before you say anything, I want you to see this," said Yasmin as she stepped closer to the girls and pulled out a sheet of paper from behind her back, holding it up for them to read. The headline read: "Daily Doings Done." All three girls moved in and began to read.

" 'Daily Doings Done,' " Jade began.

" 'My name is not Anonymous, it is Yasmin,' " continued Cloe as she read the article aloud.

" 'And I've hurt my best friends in the whole world by dishing and dissing on them,' " continued Sasha.

" 'Corrupted by fame, I turned my back on what I knew to be right, and lost myself and my friends in the process,' " Jade continued.

The girls continued reading.

" 'The Prom is gonna be off the hook, thanks to Sasha's dedication to makin' it unforgettable,' " read Sasha, satisfied.

" 'And nobody could ever say that Jade doesn't have it totally goin' on in the fashion department. Always totally stylin', she will always be two steps ahead of the rest of us, even if we don't recognize it at first,' " read Jade, her voice beginning to crack.

" 'And, as for Cameron, well, let's just say he kicked and pleaded, but we girls can be pretty persuasive. And pretty strong, too,' " Cloe read aloud. " 'He was against it from the start and it was me who set him up, not Cloe.' "

Yasmin lowered the paper. "You can read the rest in tomorrow's paper when it gets circulated. Right now, I wanted to apologize in person."

Speechless, Cloe, Sasha, and Jade continued to listen.

"I am soooooooo sorry," said Yasmin. "When the

column first came out and people thought it was boring, I wanted to spice it up. Then, when everyone started talking about it, I felt . . . important."

"Yasmin, you are important," interrupted Cloe.

"To each of us," added Jade.

"You're our friend," Sasha declared.

Yasmin continued. "I didn't think those things were going to hurt your feelings. I guess I got carried away and didn't think at all." Yasmin paused and looked at each of her friends. "Please forgive me."

Immediately, the girls embraced Yasmin.

"Of course we forgive you," said Cloe.

"We're sorry we said your column was boring," added Jade.

"We're glad you're here," whispered Sasha.

The group squeezed one another tight.

"Thank you, guys. And I'll never write another thing that I wouldn't be proud to put my name on," declared Yasmin.

Suddenly, Cloe gasped. "Oh, no. We forgot about Cameron!"

"You've got to come clean to him, Yas. He was so hurt by that picture," said Sasha.

"Cameron's gonna hate me," winced Yasmin.

"Maybe he'll understand if you apologize," Sasha said.

"He's a really great guy," confirmed Cloe.

"You're right. I'll tell him how sorry I am and convince him he just has to come to the Prom with us!"

"But before you go," Jade said, secretly picking up a bowl of spa mud and hiding it behind her. "I think you need to relax and beautify, girl!" Jade whipped the bowl of mud from behind her, and Cloe and Sasha, taking the hint, each grabbed a handful and gushed it onto Yasmin's face.

"Mud pack!" the girls screamed as Yasmin broke into hysterics.

The girls were back together, just in time for Prom.

chapter ten

It was a long time coming, but the sound of hair-dryers signaled its arrival. That and the rockin' music that was amped up to level ten on the nearby stereo. At two hours before the official start, Prom Night was here. The time had finally come to get the party started. And it was time to do it up in style. Jade, wanting to capture the start of the evening more for herself and her friends than for Mr. Del Rio, grabbed the video camera and flicked it on.

"Okay, girls, smile for the camera!" yelled Jade as she positioned the camera on her scampering friends.

"Hold up!" screamed Cloe. "I'm not fully dressed!"

Jade laughed. "Relax, I promise to keep it G-rated!"

"I'm glad Cameron took your apology okay, Yas," shouted Sasha over the music as she began to apply a touch of mascara to her gorgeous brown eyes.

Yasmin held her Prom dress up to the mirror and

smiled. "He was totally cool about everything once I said how sorry I was." Yasmin leaned in to Sasha and began to whisper. "Personally, I think he was relieved that he didn't have to blame Cloe anymore."

Sasha nodded, knowing what Yasmin was hinting at. And then she smiled.

"Gimme that camera, Jade," Cloe said. "I think the time has come for us to hit the fashion runway!"

"Fashion show!" shouted Yasmin, Sasha, and Jade in unison as they each ran to the top of the stairway, grabbing a few fashion makeover goodies on the way.

"Gimme a minute," said Cloe as she set the camera on the nearby counter, positioning the lens so it picked up the staircase. As soon as it was in place, she ran up the stairs to join her friends.

"Ready, set, go!" declared Yasmin from the top of the stairs, music blaring in the background.

Slowly, yet with a certain cutesy bounce in her step, Jade made her way down the stairs. She was dressed in a dazzling orange gown that sparkled and shined. But it was the fuzzy-feel faux fur at her waist that captured the fashion forward essence of Jade at her best. If there was any real concern that Jade had truly lost her fashion sense, all was forgotten instantly with one glance at her. With subtle make-up highlights and hair pulled up, Jade looked radiant.

Next came Sasha, dressed in a midnight-blue gown. Sequined for shimmer and glimmer, Sasha looked like a rising star, complete with light-red blush highlights and perfect-looking pink lip gloss. Her hair was pulled up with strands of hair falling from all sides, looking almost like a halo in the light. Funkadelic, yet glitzy and capturing the glamour of a timeless matinee idol, she was sure to turn heads at the Prom and make every guy wish for a dance with her.

Yasmin began her walk hesitantly, looking unsure of where to step as she descended the stairway. But as she made it halfway down, an assuredness and confidence took over as she began a sexy swagger. Radiant beyond words, Yasmin was without a doubt the Pretty Princess her friends made her out to be. Her silky blue gown was accented by a stunning hand-sewn floral design, capturing all of the mysterious finesse of the great mystery writer she had turned out to be.

As if making the entrance of a lifetime, Cloe floated down the stairs in a chalk-gray and black velvety number that reflected true sophistication in her blue eyes. With hair up and make-up glittering, she truly looked like an angel who had come down from heaven for a visit. As she reached the bottom stair, she waved directly into the camera in true Cloe fashion.

This was it, the girls were now ready. And as if on cue, a familiar *beep-beep* sounded from Cloe's driveway: Cameron had arrived with Cloe's cruiser.

"They're here!" screamed Cloe.

"Jade, grab the camera!" said Yasmin.

"Okay. Let's do it," responded Sasha as Cloe approached her front door and swung it open dramatically.

"Wow!" screamed Cloe as she gazed upon her cruiser for the first time in nearly a week, and saw that it was practically beyond recognition. "You gave my car a makeover!"

Her car looked amazing! Where once there was rust, there was now super-shiny metal. Where once there was ripped leather, there was now shiny new leather. Where once there was a dull paint job, now there was a shiny new coat. Where once there was a broken AM radio, now there was an FM radio with amped-up speakers. Where once there was a knocking sound coming from the engine, now there was only a purr. It was a totally new car, and it looked like something out of a movie. All the girls poured out of the house to check out the fixer-upper that was now fixed up. And loaded.

Losing herself in the moment, Cloe ran to Cameron and hugged him tightly. "It looks sooooooooo amazing, Cam! You did it! Thank you so much!" Cloe squealed as she pulled back and suddenly caught sight of just how good he looked in his blue-and-black tux. "You look . . . great!"

Cameron paused, not knowing what to say. "So do you, Cloe."

"And so do you!" added Cloe as she rubbed her hand along the fender of her cruiser.

Cameron cleared his throat. "Yasmin apologized

about the article and pic. I'm sorry I blamed you."

"It's okay. I understand. You were upset," said Cloe.

Yasmin, Sasha, and Jade were still checking out the car when a shiny black stretch-limo with tinted windows pulled up.

"Wow, who ordered the stretch?" asked Jade.

Suddenly, the back windows began to lower. "I told you my wheels were superstylin'!" said Dylan as he popped his head out of the limo. "But looks like you got the hook-up, as well!" From the sunroof, Dana, Meygan, and Koby popped out, waving hello. All looked totally superstylin' in their Prom outfits. And all were ready to par-tay! "Now, let's rock and roll!" Dylan said.

"Wait!" shouted Jade as she ran to the side of the stretch and handed Koby the camera. "I hope you're ready for your big break, cuz we want *you* to film us tonight!"

Koby smiled, knowing this was going to be his first reality-TV effort. "Lights, camera . . . action!" he said as he raised the camera to his eye.

"See you girls there!" declared Cameron, climbing into the limo.

Cloe switched on the radio, put on her seatbelt, and put her car into drive. "Ready, girls?" she asked Yasmin, Jade, and Sasha. The girls began to cheer as the car backed out of the driveway. This was it. The party was in full swing.

■　　■　　■　　■

Within minutes, both cars turned up the drive leading to the school. As they did, the gang caught sight of two spinning spotlights that were churning in time, back and forth.

"Sasha, this is totally class," laughed Yasmin.

"Grade A," said Cloe.

"Wait till we get inside, ladies," hinted Sasha.

The stretch, followed by the cruiser, pulled up to the school's gates. Two men in red-and-black uniforms approached both vehicles and opened the doors. Yasmin and Jade jumped out of the cruiser while Sasha and Cloe did a quick touch-up of pink lip gloss before stepping out. Dylan, with Meygan on his right arm and Dana on his left, was escorted out of the limo. Koby decided to fall back a bit to get a better shot for filming.

"Wait! Wait up, everybody!" Sasha declared as she ran to the head of the group. "We have to make the coolest entrance Stiles High has ever seen!"

"Yeah! This is our moment to shine!" shouted Jade.

Cloe turned to Cameron. "Are you ready?"

"Lead the way, ladies," responded Cameron, now more eager than ever for the fun to begin.

Koby raised the camera up to his eye. "It was a night they had all waited patiently for," he began as the girls and boys made their way up the red carpet, through the archway of balloons and streamers, and into the vast gymnasium. "It was a night they would never, ever . . ." Koby suddenly stopped short and gasped in horror. ". . . forget." He lowered the camera and stood there, dumb-founded.

"What's going on?" whispered Sasha in disbelief as she scanned the gym. The Prom was a disaster! Everything was wrong. There were no finger foods or drinks. There was no fashion photographer taking pictures of the couples. There were no groovin' tunes playing. There was nothing. All of the gym lights were on full blast, as if a basketball game was about to begin. And all of the students, decked out in the coolest threads, were standing around, confused and bewildered.

This cannot be happening, Sasha thought. Was she dreaming? Everything was all set, just yesterday. How could this be? Good friends Nevra and Eitan emerged from the crowd and ran up to her.

"Sasha, the photographer just called," said Nevra. "He's quitting the photo business to become a painter. He said sorry."

"What?! Sorry doesn't cut it! Where's DJ Chip-Chop?" asked Sasha frantically.

"In bed with the flu," responded Eitan.

"Are you kidding? What about the caterers? Did they cancel, too?"

"Nope," said Nevra.

"Thank goodness," replied Sasha.

"But they're stuck in traffic and won't be here for two hours!" continued Nevra.

"Oh, man," Sasha sighed. "Looks like your column got one thing right, Yasmin. This Prom is sad!"

"No way! My column was wrong!" Yasmin assured her. "We are gonna take care of this . . . now!"

Yasmin turned to Cloe. "Our camera can take digital stills for the Prom pictures. You and Koby go," she said as she directed them where to set up.

"And a party's not a party without some of my famous chips and guacamole, right?" offered Yasmin.

"Food run!" Dylan yelled as he grabbed Yasmin's hand and began escorting her out. "We'll take the limo."

"I'll fire up that disco ball and fill up the dance floor with balloons!" announced Jade as she grabbed a few onlookers for help. "And, Sasha, who are you kidding?" Jade turned to her friend. "You never go anywhere without your tunes!"

"That DJ booth is ours!" shouted Eitan.

"I've got the perfect beats in my locker!" answered Sasha as she and Eitan dashed in the direction of the class-rooms.

The gang had come too far to let it fall apart. Only by working together could they pull it off. The time was now.

chapter eleven

Sasha's jumping music and Eitan's mixing effects were the first signs that things were picking up. Next came the flash of the digital camera Koby was holding while Cameron and Cloe set up romantic portraits for the Prom attendees. And then there were the mounds of munchies that were spread out over several tables, compliments of Yasmin and Dylan. And, finally, the balloons and streamers that Jade, Meygan, and Dana set up around the crazy-cool catwalk gave it the look that everybody had hoped for. But it was all the students laughing and having fun that was the real indication that the party had taken off. It took exactly forty-five minutes for everything to come full swing, but it was better than it had ever been, because everybody had worked together to make it happen.

"Whew! This do-it-yourself Prom gig turned out alright!" Jade yelled to Dana over the music as they headed for the refreshment table.

"Sure did! This party's super-slammin!" agreed Dana.

Meygan, passing with the Prom King and Queen ballot box, stopped by to tease her friends with some info. "And all the votes for Prom King and Queen have been counted. Get ready!"

Jade and Dana looked at each other in anticipation.

"Who do you think?" asked Dana.

"I guess we'll find out soon enough!" responded Jade with a smile on her face.

Across the gym, Koby approached Yasmin at the refreshment stand and put the video camera up to his eye. "So, you're the infamous Anonymous, huh, Yasmin?"

"I was. But that's all behind me," said Yasmin, speaking directly into the camera.

Koby continued. "So, you're not planning any more articles, then?"

"You know, I do have one more scoop," Yasmin declared as she lifted up her hands to announce the head-line of her future article. " 'Stiles Students Save Prom in

Style!' Has a ring to it, dont'cha think?" Koby smiled.

Suddenly, the high-pitched sound of audio feedback reverberated across the gym. All of the students covered their ears and turned to see a slightly overweight and befuddled man at the podium on the runway stage. It was the "Principal with Principles" himself, Principal Mellman, and he was about to make an announcement.

"Ahhhhhh . . . hello?" started Mr. Mellman. "If I may have your attention, students. Well, it's the moment we've all been waiting for! Time to crown the Prom King and Queen of Stiles High!"

The girls nervously looked at one another.

Mr. Mellman began to open the envelope as a drumroll began to sound. The crowd was silent. "Your votes have been tallied, and your Prom King is . . . Dylan!"

The crowd broke into huge cheers as Cloe, Yasmin, Jade, and Sasha looked at one another and smiled. They knew that the usually arrogant Dylan was now going to be i-m-p-o-s-s-i-b-l-e! As huge colorful lights began to swirl, and a funky tune began to play, Dylan leaped up and onto the stage. The look on his smug face said it all as he was crowned King. Grabbing the microphone from Mr. Mellman, Dylan turned to the cheering crowd as his crown was placed atop his head.

"Stiles High," Dylan began, with scepter in hand. "I always knew you had great taste. I look forward to serving you as your King!"

Jade covered her face in embarrassment, not for herself, but for Dylan, as the crowd continued to cheer. *What a total dope*, she thought.

Grabbing the microphone from Dylan, Mr. Mellman continued. "And . . . your Prom Queen is . . ." The entire student body fell silent once again. Cloe, Yasmin, Sasha, and Jade held their breath in anticipation. "Jade!" shouted Mr. Mellman as the spotlight fell directly on Jade.

"He didn't just say 'Jade,' did he?" Jade asked her friends, who responded by leading her up to the podium. Koby rushed in to capture a close-up of the event with his video camera.

"Well, if you still think you've lost your fashion sense . . . no one else at Stiles High does!" yelled Cloe as Jade was hoisted up onto the runway stage.

With flashbulbs going off in every direction and the audience now chanting her name, Jade made her way to the center of the stage as she was crowned Prom Queen. She definitely felt redeemed as she approached the microphone to address the audience. "You like me, you really like me!" she screamed. The audience cheered and clapped.

Dylan then grabbed Jade's arm and they both began to walk the catwalk. As they made their way around, the crowd continued to shout and chant their names. Jade caught sight of Cloe and Cameron on the dance floor and gave a little wave.

"You know what the best part of this week has been?" Cloe shouted as she turned to Cameron.

"What?" asked Cameron, suddenly lost in her eyes.

"I said, you know what the best part of this week has been?" shouted Cloe louder, thinking Cameron hadn't heard her.

"Yeah, no, I heard you the first time. I meant, 'what?' What's the best part?"

Both Cameron and Cloe giggled nervously.

"Noticing new things about old friends and

learning to appreciate what was always there," Cloe said.

"That's cool!" responded Cameron.

"And that includes you. I really like that we're getting to know each other better. And I'm so glad that you decided to come to the Prom, after all!" Cloe continued.

"Me, too," responded Cameron as the music suddenly switched over to a very slow jam. Cloe and Cameron smiled awkwardly at each other. "Do you . . . want . . . to dance?" asked Cameron.

"You bet!" responded Cloe as she slowly placed her arms around Cameron's neck. Feeling his face begin to flush, Cameron pulled her close and they began to rock gently.

From a distance away, Sasha and Yasmin caught sight of Cameron and Cloe and began to smile.

"How cute they look," whispered Yasmin dreamily.

"I always knew there was something goin' on there," announced Sasha.

As they danced, Cloe rested her head on Cameron's shoulder. Cameron smiled, knowing this was a moment he would never forget. As he did, he briefly caught sight of his reflection only a foot away in what looked to be a video lens. Koby's video camera was now directly pointed at both him and Cloe.

"Koby, scram!" barked Cameron.

"Hey!" said Cloe. "Kill the camera, Koby!"

"But this is the good stuff," Koby protested.

"Take it someplace else," said Cameron.

"And so ends perhaps the greatest film Stiles High has ever produced," Koby continued as he scooted away from the couple, now turning the camera toward his own face and continuing. "The road to the Prom has been a bumpy one. But it has been a road paved with dreams and desires."

Suddenly, the music switched over to a faster beat, and Koby turned his attention to the dance floor. As he did, he saw the whole gang dancing it up, laughing and having what looked to be the time of their lives. Seeing this, Koby felt the funk deep within. "Oh . . . I always wanted to be an actor, anyway!" whispered Koby under his breath as he lowered the camera. He turned to Mr. Mellman, who was now only a few feet away. "Mr. Mellman, I need you to shoot me partying with my friends!"

"Uh . . . well . . . sure, Koby," responded Mr. Mellman, remembering that Koby was the guy who helped make him famous.

Koby quickly showed Mr. Mellman the basics and then ran out to the dance floor to groove with his friends. The gang danced and danced. This was it: Prom Night was a smash. It had been quite a crazy road, but through teamwork and friendship, it had worked out. Big-time.

"What a night!" yelled Cloe over the funky music. "Way to go, Sasha. Miss Prom Committee Chair!"

"Thanks, but it took everyone chipping in to make this Prom the bomb," responded Sasha graciously.

"I'm so glad to have funky friends like you!" shouted Yasmin as the three girls hugged one another.

Jade, finished with paying her respects to the Prom court, made her way to the girls out on the dance floor. "Now, how does it feel to be basking in the presence of a Prom Queen?" she asked in an over-the-top manner.

"It royally rules, your highness!" responded Cloe, curtseying to the Queen.

"How long does the Queen get to rule for, anyway?" asked Dana.

"As long as she wants!" squealed Jade in excitement.

"Hey, girls!" Meygan shouted. "Express yourself!"

Cloe, Yasmin, Jade, and Sasha turned to Mr. Mellman, who was still holding the camera, and struck superstylin' poses. Feeling so good, they looked absolutely radiant. It was one night they knew they would never forget, not simply for how perfect it was, but for everything it had taken to make it happen.

chapter twelve

On Monday morning, Mr. Del Rio and the class sat silently watching the very personal video assignment the girls had put together. *Keepin' It Real*, they called it, not only because it was a reality-TV video, but because they wanted to show it as they really lived it, both the good times and the bad. And thanks to Koby's editing skills, the girls were able to pull together all the footage they had captured into a cohesive, true-to-life twenty-five-minute video.

As the girls watched the video, they were all reminded of the crazy week it had been and how lucky they were to have one another. Cloe thought of her car crash and thanked the stars once again that she and her friends weren't injured.

Jade sat contemplating the big issue of personal integrity and being true to one's heart, even if it means risking ridicule. She realized that sometimes being one step ahead means waiting for others to catch up. It was that simple.

Sasha was moved as she watched her friends pull together to make the Prom what it was: the coolest night of the year. Always the girl who liked to be in control, she learned that, sometimes, you need to turn to others for help.

And as Yasmin sat watching the video, she turned her attention down to her desk. On it sat the latest edition of the *Stiles Shout-Out!* with her "Daily Doings" apology plastered across the front. She would never compromise herself or her friends ever again to get ahead. And she was lucky to have such understanding and wonderful friends.

As the end credits rolled on the video, the class clapped and a few even cheered. But Mr. Del Rio, at the far side of the room, stared blankly at the television. The girls looked at one another. What would happen if he hated it? Not only would they fail the class, and probably be grounded for the whole summer, but it would mean that they had revealed their private and personal sides to the whole class . . . for nothing! Thinking of that made Sasha feel sick.

Slowly, Mr. Del Rio rose from his desk chair and approached the front of the class. "Well," he began, clearing his throat. "You girls have certainly taken a very original approach to my art assignment."

That was it. The girls knew he hated it. Why else would he be searching for something to say? Cloe sank in her seat. Jade put her head on her desk. Sasha looked out the nearby window. And Yasmin grabbed the newspaper and pretended she was reading.

But, suddenly, Mr. Del Rio's grave tone became filled with warmth. "And I, for one, loooooooovvveeedd it!" Hearing this, the students broke out into cheers. Cloe, Yasmin, Sasha, and Jade looked to one another and beamed. "It was original, captivating, stylish, and told me so much about each one of you." Turning to grab a piece of chalk, Mr. Del Rio proceeded to write a huge A+ on the blackboard. "Congratulations, girls! You're all getting A-pluses!"

The girls jumped up out of their seats and

high-fived one another as Mr. Del Rio and the class began to clap. They were on top of the world, and they felt like superstars. It was the perfect ending to such a crazy week. And a perfect ending to the school year. Now it was time for a sun-kissed summer.